Also available from Warbranch Press, Inc.:

A GRACIOUS PLENTY

written and illustrated by
Kate Salley Palmer

and

The Pink House

written and illustrated by
Kate Salley Palmer

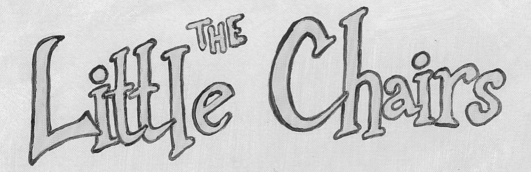

The Little Chairs

Warbranch Press, Inc.

Published by Warbranch Press, Inc.
329 Warbranch Road/Central, SC 29630

ISBN   0-9667114-2-4

Published by Warbranch Press, Inc.
329 Warbranch Road
Central, SC 29630
First Printing

for
Myrtis
and
Billy

Once there was a mama and a daddy who loved each other very much.
Every day, they went to their jobs and they came home.

They mowed their grass and pulled weeds out of their flowers.

They cooked their supper and ate together.

They watched TV.

On pretty days, they took rides through the country in their car.

One day after work, the mama
found the daddy sitting quietly
in a dark corner. And sunshine
going to waste outdoors.

The daddy sat there all evening.
He didn't turn on the light.

He didn't feel like talking,
He said.

He didn't feel like eating.
All he felt was sad, he said.
Very sad.

The mama was frightened. "What is making you sad?" She asked.
"Did I do something to make you sad?"

"No," sighed the daddy, "I think I am making myself sad. And I don't know how to stop it."

The grass in the yard grew tall and bushy.

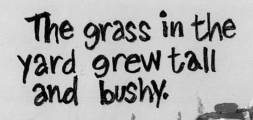

Suppers were lonely.

The TV hardly ever got watched.

There were no more rides through the country.

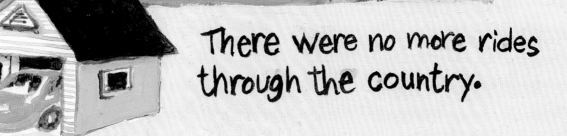

The mama wanted to help the daddy, whom she loved.
But she had not made him sad.
And she couldn't make him happy again.

Still, she wanted to help him
stop sitting alone in the dark
with pretty days gone to waste.

One day, after work, the mama
showed the daddy a little wooden chair.

"I need your help," she said.

"I can't help you," said the daddy. "I'm too tired. I just want to sit here."

"But I need you," she told him. "You can be a lot of help. Do you see this little chair?"

"Yes," said the daddy.

"I need you to paint this chair. Paint it yellow, for the front porch?" The mama showed the daddy a large can of yellow paint.

The daddy looked at the little chair. He looked at the paint. "That is easy enough, painting a chair," he said. "Maybe I can do that. If you really need me."

"I really need you," said the mama.

So the daddy took the chair, a small paintbrush, and the large can of yellow paint. He went out back to the screened porch.

There were old newspapers spread all over the porch floor. He wiped the chair clean.

He dipped the paintbrush into the yellow paint.

The bright color made him think of a summer day's sunshine. And butterfly wings. And a puppy he once had. His eyes followed each movement as he brushed the color onto the wood.

When the chair was covered all over with bright yellow, the daddy called the mama to look at it.

The mama looked at the daddy. "Paint it again?" she said.

"Again?" asked the daddy.

"Yes, don't you think it needs another coat?" asked the mama.

The daddy thought. He thought about how smoothly the paint flowed from the brush, and how bright the color looked.

"Yes," he agreed. "It needs another coat."

The next day the daddy came home from work and sat once again in his dark place.
The mama came to him and said,
"Here is another little chair. I need you to paint this one blue."

The daddy thought about the little yellow chair.
He remembered how smoothly the paint flowed from the brush and how bright the color looked.
"Okay, I guess I can paint another chair," he said. He got the new little chair.

And he went out to the back porch.

There was the first little chair on yesterday's newspapers, with two coats of yesterday's yellow.

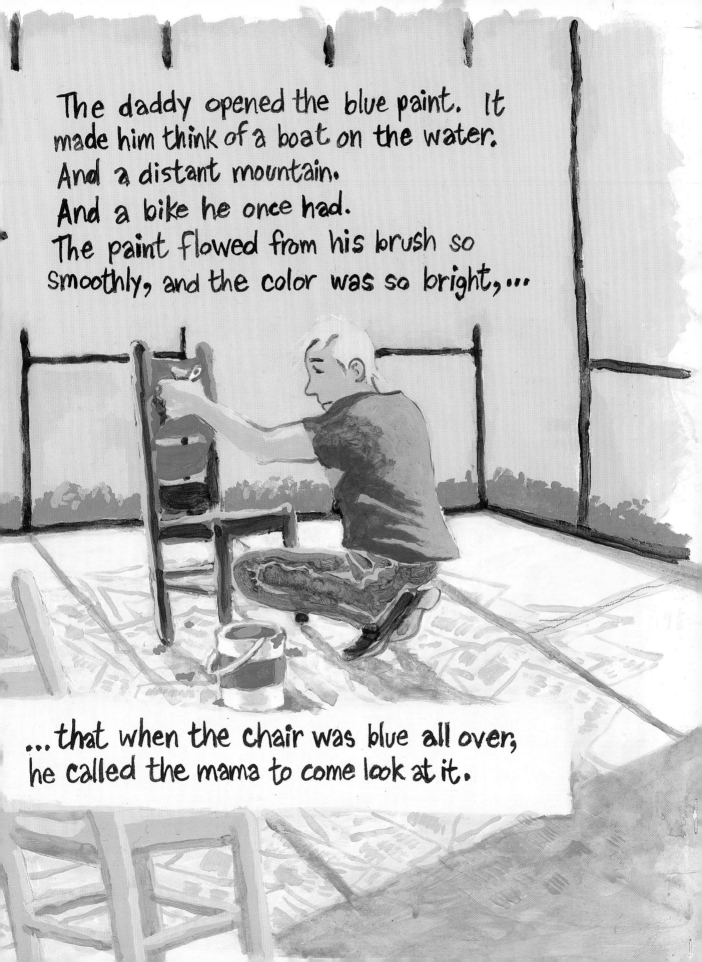

The daddy opened the blue paint. It made him think of a boat on the water. And a distant mountain. And a bike he once had. The paint flowed from his brush so smoothly, and the color was so bright,...

...that when the chair was blue all over, he called the mama to come look at it.

The daddy thought. He thought about how smoothly the paint flowed from the brush and how bright the color looked.

"Okay," he agreed, "I'll paint it again." And he did.

The daddy felt lucky to have a wife who needed him to do a job like this. A job with smooth paint flowing and colors so bright.

"The more the merrier," he said.

He opened the paint. It looked like apples and flags and Christmas bows and lipstick kisses.

When he finished, he painted the chair all over again! Then he called the mama to come look at it.

The next day, the daddy found another little chair on the screen porch- and a can of paint as green as Springtime!

He covered the new little chair with green paint until it was shining like trees after a storm.